THE
BOY
WHO
LOST
HIS
SPARK

For Juno Aphra,
with love – M.O'F.

For Rudy, Juniper and Nat,
for their perfect acting and patient posing – D.J.T.

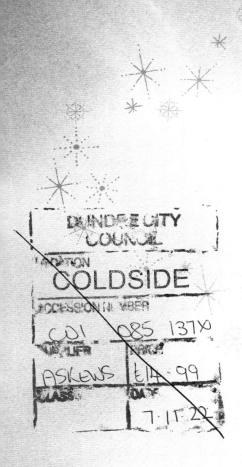

First published 2022 by Walker Books Ltd
87 Vauxhall Walk, London SE11 5HJ

2 4 6 8 10 9 7 5 3 1

Text © 2022 Maggie O'Farrell
Illustrations © 2022 Daniela Jaglenka Terrazzini

Lyrics for "Song of the Nouka" by Maggie O'Farrell
Music for "Song of the Nouka" arranged by Paddy Tunney based on an old Irish jig:
"An Seanduine Dóite" or "The Burnt Old Man"

The right of Maggie O'Farrell and Daniela Jaglenka Terrazzini to be identified as
the author and illustrator respectively of this work has been asserted
in accordance with the Copyright, Designs and Patents Act 1988

This book has been typeset in Baskerville

Printed in Italy

British Library Cataloguing in Publication Data:
a catalogue record for this book is available from the British Library

ISBN 978-1-4063-9201-2

www.walker.co.uk

THE
BOY
WHO
LOST
HIS
SPARK

by

MAGGIE O'FARRELL

illustrated by

DANIELA JAGLENKA TERRAZZINI

WALKER BOOKS
AND SUBSIDIARIES
LONDON · BOSTON · SYDNEY · AUCKLAND

Has anything strange ever
happened in your house?

When Jem's mother sold their flat in
the city and moved them to a cottage
on the steep side of a hill, it wasn't long
before peculiar things began to occur.

Jem discovered his shoes, left by the back door, mysteriously filled up with conkers. His mother opened the washing machine one day to find that the cheese grater had found its way into the laundry, and now their shirts and socks and jumpers were shredded and torn. A week after that, Jem went into the kitchen and saw that all the cupboards had been taped shut, so that he couldn't get out the plates for dinner.

And then came the morning when a ball of wool from the knitting basket had been wound around and around the banisters: back and forth the strands went, crazily and wonkily, like a woollen web across the stairs.

Jem sat down with a thud on the top step. Their mother climbed carefully through the yarn, saying that she would fetch some scissors. Verity, Jem's sister, clasped her hands together and said, with shining eyes: "I think a nouka was here last night."

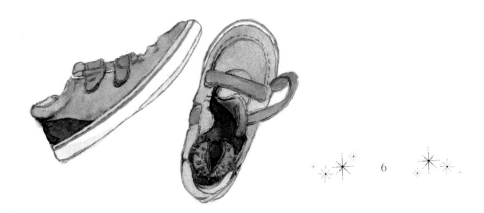

Jem buried his head in his arms and sighed. Ever since the move, Verity had been obsessed with an imaginary creature called the 'nouka'. On her very first day at their new school, her class had been told an old folk tale about little creatures who used to live inside the hill, occasionally coming out to cause mischief. Verity had loved the story and had been digging holes all over the garden, trying to see if she could find one. Not so long ago, Jem would have picked up a spade and joined her but lately he hadn't felt like it; it was as if someone had put misted-up glasses on his face and he could no longer see the fun or the magic in Verity's games. He missed their flat, he missed the city – its yellow pools of streetlights, the trams that used to rattle past at night. He felt so low and listless, sitting there, as if his insides had been stuffed with damp rags.

Instead of telling his mother and sister this, it seemed easier to stand up, fight his way through the woollen maze and shout: "I'm tired of hearing about the stupid nouka. There's no such thing!"

Jem stamped out of the front door, across the garden, and climbed the oak tree.

He had never been up here before. The branches holding him were twisted and strong, reaching out like encircling arms. A thick fleece of leaves surrounded Jem on all sides, shielding him from the world. He found a fork where two boughs met and he sat down, rubbing his fingertips against the rippled, ridged bark that resembled the overlapping scales of a seamonster. Hooking his feet around the trunk, he gazed at this surprising secret space, feeling the way it rocked slightly, a great, green ship in the wind.

Through the fluttering leaves, Jem could see glimpses of the hill. It was high and sheer, with one side shaped like a forehead, the other the craggy tail of a dragon. Trees grew around its base and halfway up was a small, silver lake that sometimes caught the reflections of clouds within its banks. On sunny days, the hill cast a blue-tinged replica of itself to the ground.

Jem was seized with an urge to sprint up it, to hide himself among its yellow gorse bushes and waving bracken, and never come down again. He could live up there, all on his own, and he'd never have to listen to conversations about underground creatures or do homework or be asked to move house.

He knew, however, that someone would come and find him and here, now, was his mother, coming out of the cottage, handing up a plate of hot, buttered toast.

"Don't be too hard on your sister, Jem," his mother murmured, putting a hand on his ankle.

"But she's always doing annoying stuff – covering the stairs with wool and filling shoes with conkers," Jem blurted out, through a mouthful of toast, "and then blaming it on this … creature. And there's no such thing as the nouka. You know that, I kn—"

He was interrupted by a curious sound from somewhere at the base of the tree: a rustling, a scuffling, like the beating of a wing or the rub of fur against rock. Jem frowned and clutched at a branch for balance.

"Did you hear that?" he demanded.

"What?"

"That noise."

"I heard something," said his mother, glancing around. "It was probably just the cat." Then she squeezed his foot. "Jem, I know it's been hard for you, moving here, and leaving all your friends behind but—"

"I'm fine," Jem said, curling his hands into themselves.

"If you ever want to chat about—"

"I don't."

Jem shut his eyes. He didn't want to talk or even think about the flat where he had lived all his life. He didn't want to remember the windowseat where he used to sit and watch people coming and going on the pavements below. Or the door where pencil marks were made on his and Verity's birthdays, showing how much they had grown. To think about the flat without them in it made terrible feelings swell inside him. How could another family be living there now? Had they kept the pencil marks or rubbed them away? Whenever these thoughts rose up in him, he had to squash them down somewhere dark and small inside him.

"I'm fine," he said again, but when he opened his eyes, his mother was looking at him with a gaze that wasn't fooled at all.

"Time to go, Jem," she said, glancing at her watch. "Down you come."

On the way to school, Verity was quiet. Jem walked with her along the path that led from their cottage, up and over the hill, to the village on the other side. He waited, as patiently as he could, when she ducked down to peer into each and every rabbit warren, when she examined the path for tiny footprints. Usually, Verity would chatter the whole way, telling him how she planned to find a nouka, but today she barely said a word.

"What's up?" Jem asked, nudging her. And, remembering that he had been unkind, he reached out and took her schoolbag, shrugging it onto his own shoulder, by way of an apology.

She bent to look into a narrow hole, saying something
so softly he had to ask her to repeat it.

"I said," Verity whispered, still gazing into the earth,
"that you shouldn't have said that about noukas."

"That they don't exist?"

"Shh," Verity said, glancing around her, as if a band of indignant creatures might at any moment burst from the hill.

Jem tried not to laugh. "What will they do if they hear me? Come and teach me a lesson?"

Verity regarded him gravely. "Don't, Jem," she said, in a voice so sad it squeezed Jem's heart. "I really want to see one. And if you're mean about them, they might not come."

"Sorry." Jem took her small hand in his own and, to humour her, asked, "What do they look like? Did your teacher say, when she told you about the legend?"

"It wasn't the teacher who told us. It was the old lady."

"What old lady?"

"The one with white hair. Have you seen her? She lives in the house next to school. She used to be a teacher, a long time ago, and she comes, once a week, to tell us stories."

"Well, did she say what they looked like?"

"Little and fluffy," Verity said, cupping her hands, as if she was picturing a nouka contained within them, "with black fur that sticks out all around. Unless it's been raining – water makes their fur go droopy."

"Oh."

"Noukas hate rain. She said that, in the olden days, when noukas lived in the hill, the people in the village knew that no mischief would happen on rainy days because noukas don't come out when it's wet."

Jem decided he'd had enough of this conversation and began to walk faster. "We should hurry," he said. "Or we'll be late for school. Come on, I'll race you."

And on they ran, laughing, down the side of the hill, just in time to hear the school bell.

THE FIRST LESSON OF THE DAY WAS ABOUT volcanoes. Jem's teacher, Mr Shale, drew a diagram on the board, showing them how lava would build up inside until the pressure and heat became too much.

Jem, I'm sorry to say, did not like school very much. Sitting at a desk for hours was terribly hard for him; he had no idea how other children managed it so effortlessly.

His feet and hands liked to keep moving. There had been times, at his old school, when he tilted his chair so far back that he and the chair had parted company and he had fallen to the floor. The teacher there hadn't liked Jem, and called him a 'troublemaker'. Jem was trying very hard to curb his restlessness, and to keep on the good side of his new teacher.

The real problem, however, was that numbers and letters wouldn't behave for him, as they did for other people: letters refused to line up into proper words, numbers tended to run away and hide. This, Jem knew, was going to be harder to conceal. A pen in Jem's hand seemed to prefer drawing griffins or goblins instead of writing sentences or doing sums. Ink got all over his fingers and then his clothes, so that at the end of the day he was covered in dark smuts and smudges.

Today's lesson, however, he did like. He drew his own volcano, giving it steep sides and a large chamber for the lava. He was just about to make it explode, with billows of smoke and ash, when the teacher said something that made Jem look up.

"And our very own hill," Mr Shale was saying, "was once a volcano, many thousands of years ago."

Astounded, Jem looked out of the window. He looked at the diagram on the board. He looked back at Mr Shale. He put up his hand.

"Is that true?" he asked. "That our hill is a volcano?"

"Was," Mr Shale corrected, with a smile, "a long time ago. But its fire has long since gone out."

"Did it explode and spurt lava everywhere?" Jem asked.

"Probably," said Mr Shale, who was, to Jem's dismay, writing out a long division sum on the board. Then he stopped and turned round. "Bear in mind, Jem," he said, "that anything else you might hear about our hill is not true. It was a volcano but now it's just a hill. There is nothing inside it but rock and rock and more rock."

Jem stared. Mr Shale couldn't be referring to the legend of the nouka. Could he? All around Jem was the noise of his classmates picking up pencils to start their sums but Jem sat, motionless. He swivelled his eyes towards the hulk of the hill. He tried to picture it as it once was: a volcano, slopes alive with molten movement, summit spurting fire and ash, its centre aflame.

Jem put up his hand again.

"If the hill used to be a volcano, then how—?"

"Jem," Mr Shale interrupted, "you need to begin your maths. And do please try not to fidget. You'll fall off your chair if you're not careful."

"Could it be possible that—?"

"Maths, Jem." The normally kind teacher was beginning to frown.

"But what if—?"

"Enough. Get on with your work."

Jem did not mean to be naughty. It was just that, sometimes, it was hard to be good.

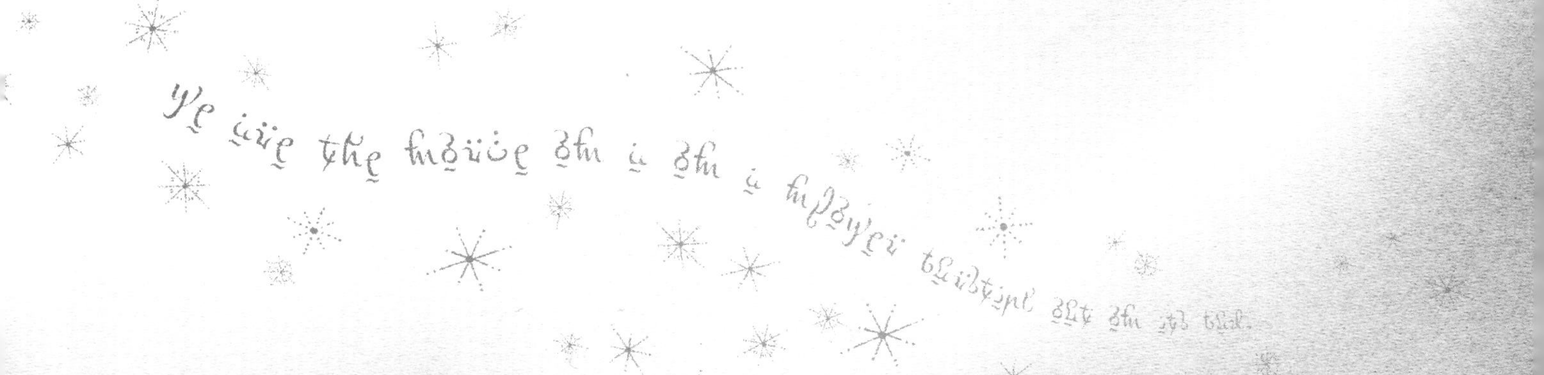

On his way home, Jem passed the house next to the school and there was the old woman with white hair. She was sitting in a chair on her doorstep, a book in her lap. Her fingers were gnarled like tree roots and her face was webbed with lines; Jem had heard that she was the oldest person in the village.

"Hello there," she said, when she saw Jem standing at her gate. "How's your little sister today?"

Something in her tone reminded Jem that this woman had once been a teacher. He took a wary step back. Had he done something wrong? Could she somehow look inside his head and see his trouble with letters and numbers and staying still?

"Fine," he said, gripping the strap of his schoolbag, ready to make a run for it if he needed to.

"You've moved into that cottage on the other side of the hill, haven't you?"

"Yes."

"You like it?"

Jem was silent. He didn't know how to say that he missed his old home so much that there was no room inside him to like the new place.

"You ever have any trouble there?"

"No," he said, quickly.

The old woman regarded him over her spectacles for a long moment. "Good," she said. "If you ever do, just leave a little something outside your back door."

Jem stared at her. "Pardon?"

"A bowl of porridge or a few crusts. It keeps them happy, you see."

"Who?"

"You know who."

Jem drew himself up to his full height and, remembering Mr Shale's words, said: "There is nothing inside that hill but rock and rock and more rock."

The old woman raised her eyebrows but said nothing. Jem took in the hands lying on the open book, the piercing gaze behind the spectacles, then he turned and ran. He ran through the streets, along the path, and up the side of the hill.

"There is nothing here!" he shouted. "Nothing at all! I don't believe in the nouka! I don't, I don't, I don't."

The hill took in his words. It accepted them. It let them filter down into its ancient volcanic depths. For a moment, all was quiet and still. Then a breeze seemed to stir up from nowhere, ruffling the bracken, rustling the leaves, and the trees seemed to sigh and shake their heads at him.

Jem bolted down the path, towards home.

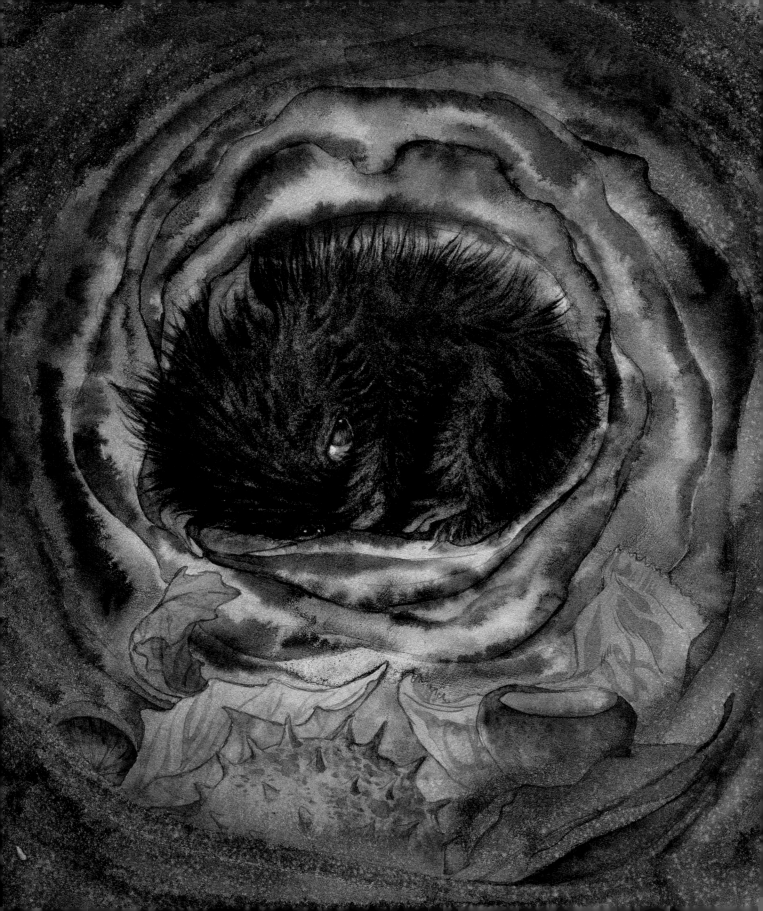

BENEATH THE GRASS, BENEATH THE SOIL, through the layers and layers of rock, deep down inside the hill, something woke.

In the thick, velvet dark, a pair of green eyes flickered opened, fell shut, then opened again. The creature's face was tucked under its arm, nose buried in fur for warmth. It wasn't ready to wake up. It yawned then resolutely curled itself up more tightly, drawing in all its limbs so that it resembled a black powder-puff. Whatever had woken it could wait.

THUMP, THUMP, THUMP.

A small frown pleated the furry brow. One eye opened and looked up at the rocky ceiling.

THUMP, THUMP,
BANG,
CRASH.

It let out a little yip of dismay. Something, or someone, appeared to be running over its hill, with emphatic, angry strides. Reverberations were travelling down through the soil and rocks and walls and passages. The soft triangular ears on its head twitched forwards then back. There was to be no more sleep today, it could see. So it stretched one paw, then another, rolled over and stood up.

It was a being very attuned to what was going on around it, to what might be happening in the hearts and minds of others; its sticking-out fur acted as antennae, drawing signals from the air. Right now, it was picking up that whoever was stamping across its hill was very upset.

It didn't like unhappiness, not one bit. Contentment, the creature experienced as a spreading warmth on its paws and back; being near a happy human was like sitting in a sunbeam. But unhappiness travelled unpleasantly down its whiskers, like a prickle or an itch or the beginning of a sore throat. There had been too much unhappiness near this hill recently.

Its fur began to quiver. It brought up a paw to rub at its suddenly itchy nose. Something was being shouted up there:

I don't believe in the nouka!

The creature stopped rubbing and stood motionless, shocked, barely breathing. That feeling came into its whiskers, making them tremble at their very roots. Then it was overcome by a sneeze, again and again.

Far above, the footsteps receded, then vanished.

Jem's mother was standing in the kitchen when he got back, making dinner, still in her work clothes. Verity was in the garden, busily digging in the soil near the oak tree.

Jem sat down at the table. His homework was to finish the volcano diagram. He drew rivers of lava, great clouds of steam, and wrote the labels in the best writing he could manage.

He had a feeling that some of the letters hadn't come out in the order they were meant to, but he hoped that Mr Shale would be so impressed with the drawing that he wouldn't notice the spelling. They ate dinner and his mother went upstairs to put Verity to bed. Jem slowly dried the dishes, one by one. He didn't like the way the countryside was so unnervingly quiet. He was a child used to the background hum of traffic, sirens, and voices from other flats coming through the walls. How could it be that silence was louder than noise?

Then, for a reason unknown to him, he turned and looked out of the window at the hill. It had darker patches, but he knew that was just the bracken. It wasn't possible for such a thing as a nouka to exist. Jem knew this.

Even so, he made certain that his bedroom curtains were shut tight that night, so that not a sliver of the hill could be seen.

T HE CREATURE WAS PADDING ALONG
a passageway on velvet paws, humming a spiralling,
wordless song that was as ancient as itself.

Reaching the secret opening, it parted the grass and
bracken with its fingertips and poked its head out into
the dusk. It felt the ruffling sensation of a gentle breeze
through its fur and, raising its nose, sniffed the air.
Shoe leather, fern, freshly dug soil, laced with human
cooking smells. Pasta, and perhaps … a crumble?

Still humming, the nouka ventured out, checking
the path, the lit windows of the house. Nobody was
about. Not the boy, not the girl, not the mother. There
were signs of them – the spade left by the tree,
a teddy stranded on the swing, a mug
on the bench.

The nouka had never, of course, had a lesson about volcanoes. It hadn't, like Jem, been taught that the places where the hill's narrow tunnels met the surface were called 'vents'. It simply knew that there were several exits from the hill, and one of them was here, behind an oak tree, in the garden of what had until recently been an empty cottage.

It crossed the lawn, skipped over the path, ducked briefly behind a gooseberry bush. After giving the inside of the mug a quick, exploratory lick and shuddering at the bitter taste of coffee grounds, it made for the door, where someone had thoughtfully installed a little swinging flap, just big enough for a nouka.

Inside, the kitchen was dim and warm, filled with the scent of the recently eaten meal. A dish towel was drying on a rail, thin wisps of condensation rising

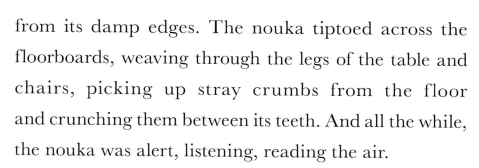

from its damp edges. The nouka tiptoed across the floorboards, weaving through the legs of the table and chairs, picking up stray crumbs from the floor and crunching them between its teeth. And all the while, the nouka was alert, listening, reading the air.

Someone in this house, it could tell, was unhappy, was the source of all the sneeze-making feelings. Someone here was sad but pretending not to be. Someone needed an outlet, a way to let off steam. Someone – and this thought made a smile curl up on its face – needed some nouka-mischief.

It edged out into the hallway, filled with glee at the task ahead, fur and whiskers bristling, its little heart thumping in its chest. It was just about to climb the stairs when it became distracted by a thought. What if the family had lit their wood-burning stove?

The nouka was extremely fond of a fire – the crack and snap of it, the orange flames licking at logs, the delicious orbit of heat, the glowing ashy embers. It very rarely got to be near one, these days. While it was looking for the person who said those terrible words, might it not be as well to sit by the hearth for a bit?

First fire, it decided, then mischief. It shivered with anticipation, swerving away from the stairs, its eager feet going pip-pap-pip on the floorboards. Fire, it was thinking, fire, fire, fire.

But when it poked its face around the living-room door, it got a horrible shock. There, inches from its nose, was a pair of legs: crossed at the ankles, feet encased in slippers. The mother was sitting in a chair with a book on her lap, blocking the way to the fire.

The nouka leapt back, fur springing up all around it in fright and, fleetingly, it was a perfectly round, sooty black ball. It darted back towards the kitchen and jumped into the cat's basket, concealing itself in the animal's fur.

After a moment, it reached out and rubbed its fingers along the gossamer-silk of the cat's neck, and began a rhythmic, spiralling tune.

The cat, Malachy, woke with a start. He had been having a lovely dream about chasing bees in a sunny garden, and now he was awake and, even worse, his ear was itching.

He brought forward first one paw to scratch it, then the other, but couldn't seem to reach. He tried to lick it and, when that didn't work, he rolled over and wriggled about on his back.

Nothing seemed to help. He could not rid himself of the itch. Malachy rose from his bed, stretched, and wandered across the kitchen, his tail held up in the shape of a question mark.

Despite knowing that it was strictly forbidden, he gave his claws a good sharpening on the arm of a chair. He poked his face into Jem's discarded schoolbag, in case it held the forgotten crust of a sandwich. Although he had already been given his dinner, something was telling him that he really should jump onto the table and see what was in that jug. This also wasn't allowed, but no one was looking and it seemed very important that he should just check.

Traces of the nouka's tune floated upwards, rising from the cat basket, twisting in the air and drifting out into the hall. The song had phrases, repeating notes, sudden sparks of melody; it spread and dispersed through the rooms of the house like the wreathing smoke from a snuffed-out candle.

When a nouka sings, it cannot be heard in the way other music can. A person might be in the same room as a crooning nouka and never be aware of it; another person might hear it as the susurration of wind through leaves, or the rattle of the lid on a boiling kettle.

The song drifted through the cottage. Upstairs, Jem heard it in a dream as the creak of his flat's front door. He turned over in his sleep, flinging out an arm towards the familiar doorknob: his alarm clock, a book and a bedside light were all swept to the floor.

In her bed, Verity, also asleep, heard it as the thud of

the oak tree dropping all its acorns in one go, and she began to wriggle, wrestling with her duvet, knocking several of her toy animals into the gap between mattress and wall.

Downstairs, Jem's mother put down her book. She had been enjoying it but now she felt suddenly restless and twitchy. The fire was hissing as it devoured its logs. She got up and paced to the window and back. Was she too hot? She yanked off her cardigan and threw it to the sofa. A moment later, she pulled it on again. She sighed and scratched her head. She decided that she must immediately rearrange all the furniture.

She was just about to push the armchair to the opposite side of the room when she was distracted by an unusual sound: a clunk, followed by a dripping. She went out of the room, across the hall and through the kitchen door.

the nasties are here.

The cat was crouched on a table mat, lapping at a sticky, sugary, yellow lake. Custard had spread from the upturned jug all over the table, oozing down onto the chairs, then the floor.

"Malachy!" she cried. "That's very naughty. What were you thinking? You don't even like custard."

Several things happened at once. Malachy, upset at being told off, darted from the room, treading sticky paw prints up the stairs. Verity woke with a start as a custardy cat sprang onto her chest. She sat up and started to shriek, getting tangled in the duvet and rolling onto the floor. Their mother came running, snapping on the light. Jem, weary and confused by all the cacophony, turned over to face the wall.

Under his bed, unseen, unnoticed, crouched a small black creature, nestling next to a balled-up sock. Its eyes were gleaming and watchful, its chin propped thoughtfully in its hands. It was looking up at the underside of Jem's mattress.

The nouka had found the
person it was looking for.

The next day, everyone was tired. Jem's alarm clock didn't go off, and the kitchen smelt of old milk, and their mother burnt the porridge, and Jem couldn't find his schoolbag. He was sure he had left it beside his bed but he eventually discovered it hanging by its strap from the oak tree, and he accused Verity of hiding it there. Verity yelled that she had done no such thing – and why was Jem being so mean? Their mother put her hands over her ears and begged them to stop. Malachy, still in disgrace, hid under the armchair.

They arrived late for school, after the bell, and Verity went off without saying goodbye.

Jem hurried along the corridor to his classroom, clattered through the door, placing his homework on Mr Shale's desk as he passed. He was proud of his volcano diagram and hoped the teacher would be pleased with it.

A slender paw extended out from the side of the hill, checking for rain. A moment later, the nouka's head appeared. It looked left and right, then up at the sky.

Wisps of white clouds were drifting across the blue, and sun was scattering golden sequins through the shifting leaves. Not a sign of rain.

Satisfied, the nouka crept out. It sidled along the wall, under the old woman's window boxes, and out into the street, keeping close to the kerb.

A car roared past, whisking the nouka's fur first one way then the other; it flattened its ears, disgruntled. Then it found a chocolate wrapper, which cheered it up again, and it snuffled its wet nose around the silver foil. A woman pushing a pushchair came around a corner; the nouka curved itself around a bollard, hiding from view. Only the baby saw it; he gave a happy shriek and opened out his star-like hands.

The nouka continued on down the street. It had lived such a long time that it could recall when this town was nothing more than a millpond, a few timber houses and a cart track. It had seen the arrival of tractors, motor cars, telephones, television aerials, houses springing up like mushrooms, washing machines, men leaving for war and some of them coming back, women discarding long dresses and large hats and taking instead to trousers.

It had seen children turn into adults, then have children of their own, and those children grow up. It had sat on its hill and watched storms and heatwaves and blizzards and droughts and floods. It knew that under a pavement near the town hall was an ancient well that could cure a cold. It knew that in a field next to the church was buried treasure – tarnished silver coins and necklaces of ruby. It knew that the corner shop used to be a dairy where it had been possible to buy cheese wrapped in leaves. It knew more about the town than anybody who lived in it.

Today, though, history was not on the nouka's mind. It trotted along, enjoying the feel of heat on its back, wondering, now that it had found the boy, how it might persuade him to stop bottling up all that sadness. The nouka bristled with pleasure at this thought, and gave a little squeak. This was its favourite kind of task. What mischief and misrule might be achieved today?

It hummed and rumbled to itself as it went, and people felt its passing, unknowingly heard its song.

The lady in the corner shop suddenly stopped stacking tins on the shelf and raised her head. She needed, she decided, to cut off all her hair and perhaps dye it blue.

A man at the counter, about to buy onions and mince, thought that perhaps he wouldn't make a pie tonight but instead he would eat ice cream for dinner. Why not?

The woman in a hallway, about to button up her beige mac, was suddenly compelled to shrug it off and find instead a silk and marabou opera cloak from her youth. She would wear it to the post office – who cared what anyone thought?

The nouka smiled to itself as it bowled along a narrow gutter, avoiding a puddle, sidestepping a pile of leaves. It came to a thoughtful stop at one of its favourite spots: the school gates.

In the classroom, the bell was ringing for breaktime and Jem was darting for the door when the teacher said, "Jem, can I have a word?"

Jem slowed, reluctantly, and went up to the teacher's desk. Mr Shale opened a homework book and pushed it towards him.

"Can you explain this?" he said.

Jem looked down. It was his diagram: there was the lava he'd drawn, the clouds of ash, the labels he'd written out so carefully. But, now, all over the hill and along the tunnels were tiny dots or scribbles. They looked like dark stars or black inkspots. Could it have been Verity? Jem felt himself filling with rage; the effort of keeping it in made the top of his head feel hot. He had really

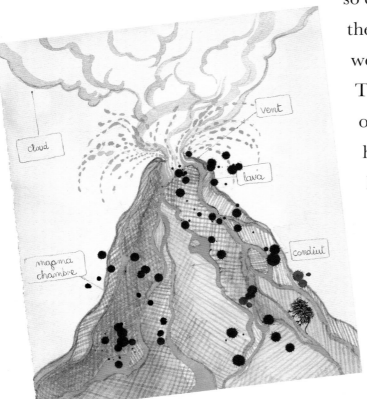

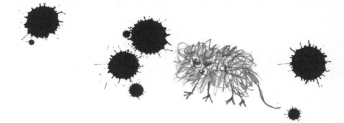

wanted to get off to a good start at this school. How could she have done this to him?

"You've drawn a beautiful picture, Jem," the teacher was saying, "a really good one. It's wonderful to see that you enjoyed the volcano lesson so much. But I'm wondering what all these little creatures are? Why did you add them?"

"I… I…" Jem stuttered. "I didn't."

Mr Shale looked down at the page, then back up. "Jem," he said, "I know it's hard, starting a new school. You're settling in so well but—"

"It wasn't me!"

"Maybe you could think about why you spoilt your lovely illustration with—"

"But I didn't," Jem insisted. "When I finished, none of those marks were there."

Mr Shale tilted his head. "Then who did?"

Jem was silent.

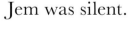

"I'm afraid," the teacher said gently, "you're going to need to stay in all breaktime, to do your diagram again. Properly, this time, please."

Jem slumped into his chair and opened his book. He looked at the inkspots or smudges or whatever they were. Swarming up the sides of the volcano, jumping off the top, travelling along the passageways of the interior. Something about them did not say Verity to him: they were too finely drawn.

Jem turned to a new page and picked up his pencil. He tried not to look outside, where his classmates were playing tag or football. He kept his eyes on the book and sketched out the shape of a new volcano: a high, triangular hill, just like the one beyond the window.

He was about to draw the ash cloud above it when he heard a chair scraping against the floor and Mr Shale's voice, saying, "What on earth?"

Jem looked up. The teacher was half-standing, staring out at the yard. Jem followed his gaze. For a moment, he couldn't tell what he was looking at. It was like a riot or a rumpus or a huge party.

Everyone was covered in crisp red and gold leaves – they were stuck to jumpers, they adhered to faces, they fell from cuffs and hems. Most shocking of all was the sight of the headmistress, a woman with a fondness for tailored suits and silk scarves, kneeling down to allow the games teacher to thread a crown of amber leaves into her hair.

"They've gone wild," Mr Shale said, in a slightly fearful whisper.

Jem looked down at the spoilt diagram, at the inkspots, some of which, he now noticed, seemed to have tiny arms and legs. He looked up at the people in the yard, then back at the diagram.

WHEN SCHOOL FINISHED, JEM WAS FIRST OUT of the door. He hurried along the road, straight to the house of the old lady. She was there, sitting in a chair on her doorstep, as usual, her hands folded in her lap. When she saw Jem, she didn't say "Hello" or "How are you?" She said, "What can I do for you?"

Jem took out the book from his bag, opened it to the page with the volcano and handed it to her without a word.

She peered at it through her glasses, and then she took them off and examined it again. "Ah," she said. "Hmm. Interesting."

"I didn't draw those … inkspot things," Jem said.

The lady touched them gently with a fingertip.

"But I got into trouble because Mr Shale thought I did."

She nodded, holding the page close to her face. "Quite an eventful day at school, I hear," she murmured.

"Yeah," Jem said. "Everyone went completely berserk."

"Do you know what my granny told me?" the woman asked. "That her granny told her that once upon a time there used to be little creatures living inside that hill. No one has seen them for a long time. People said they all went away. But I wonder if perhaps one of them got left behind."

Jem shook his head. "You can't expect me to believe that. If no one has ever seen one or—"

"Do you believe in air?" She circled a hand around her head. "The thing you breathe?"

"Of course."

"And can you see it?"

"Well, no, but—"

"There you are, then." She sat back in her chair.

Jem thought for a while, standing there on the pavement, then he asked, "Have you ever … seen one?"

The woman smiled but didn't answer. Instead, she leant forward and whispered, "They used to come down at night-time and cause mischief."

"What kind of mischief?"

"Oh, the shoelaces of the police were replaced with liquorice. The eggs in a hen's nest were painted in rainbow colours. Mud was smeared on the door handle of the grumpy shopkeeper so that he got his hands all mucky. The kinds of things we all get the urge to do but usually stop ourselves."

"Sometimes," Jem confided, "I don't stop myself."

The woman nodded, as if she knew this already.

"It used to be said that the reason why the noukas were so naughty was because they carried the spirit of the volcano within them."

"But how?" Jem said.

"Because when the final sparks of that great fiery furnace fell to the ground, they turned into creatures who would for ever be just like the volcano: unpredictable, restless, sparky. Just like we all are, every now and again. Some of us, it has to be said, more than others."

"If this," Jem gestured at his diagram, still held on the woman's lap, "is the nouka, the one who was left behind, then why? Why is it causing havoc at school? Why is it doing this to my homework?"

The woman closed the book and handed it back. She regarded him for a long moment, through her glasses. Then she said: "Maybe it decided you needed it. Maybe we all could do with a shake-up now and then, to let our wild sides take over. People have to let off steam sometimes, just like a volcano. It would never do to keep everything locked inside us, would it?"

Jem sighed. He scratched his head. He scuffed his toe against the pavement. "I don't understand," he said, eventually. "I know that lava turns into rock but how is it possible for a spark to turn into a creature? It doesn't make any sense."

The woman eased herself out of her chair. "Now isn't that," she said, picking up her watering can, "just exactly what makes life interesting – the things that don't make sense? Wouldn't life be dull if we understood everything about it?"

Then she waved a hand at him and turned towards her window boxes.

THE NOUKA WAS SITTING ON A STONE BESIDE the lake, nibbling on a blackberry, singing, trying to persuade some fish to make leaps across the surface, but the fish were pretending they couldn't hear.

Suddenly, from further down the slope came the sound of footsteps. Someone was coming along the path. The nouka nearly dropped its blackberry in fright, then it jumped down off the stone and hid behind some nettles, peering out from between their jagged leaves.

When it saw the tufty hair of the boy from the cottage, the nouka gave a pensive sniff. Here, on the hill, was the child who said he didn't believe in noukas. He was walking back from school, bag on his back, head lowered. The nouka sucked at the blackberry juice on its fingers, speculatively eyeing the boy as he kicked a stone, then caught it up, then kicked it again.

The nouka wasn't feeling very cheerful this evening. It hadn't enjoyed the rumpus at school as much as it thought it would. The sight of all those children having a riotous time together reminded it what the hill used to be like, when there were lots of other noukas to play with. And the boy's unhappiness was getting under the nouka's skin, somehow. The leaf-fight had, the nouka knew, been spectacular, but, perplexingly, it hadn't seemed to have the desired effect on this boy:

he seemed more miserable than ever. Was the nouka losing its touch, its magic? The thought made its whiskers droop.

The nouka dabbed at its eyes and started a little hum, just to cheer itself up, and on the path, two or three footsteps away, the boy stopped walking.

The nouka froze, song ceasing in its throat. Was it possible that the boy could hear it? Humans never did, at least not knowingly. But, unmistakably, the boy was turning his head from left to right, very much like someone seeking the source of a noise.

Panicking now, the nouka felt a familiar and dreaded itch invade its nose. It scrubbed at its face. Was it the blackberry? The nettles? The boy? Something was making it want to—

A-TI-SHOO!

A tiny explosion of noise echoed about the hill.

The boy took a step nearer, then another. The nouka kept itself very still, fur standing on end.

"Is anybody there?" the boy said, softly.

The nouka's eyes grew very round. It clutched the half-eaten blackberry in its paw, ears pressed flat to its head.

"Is it you? The one who drew in my book?"

To the nouka's horror, a rabbit appeared out of a nearby burrow and, on seeing the nouka, it paused, inquisitively twitching its nose. The nouka pulled a fierce face, to get it to go away, so that it didn't give away the hiding place. The rabbit took no notice, lolloping off.

On the path, the boy seemed to be thinking.

"Oh well," he said, in a clear voice that floated towards the nouka's flattened ears, "I must have been mistaken. There's nothing here, nothing inside this hill but rock. I should probably go."

He took a few steps, and said, over his shoulder, "Here I am, going home. I'm leaving now. I'm off. Goodbye, hill. Goodbye, rock."

The nouka watched as the boy disappeared around a bend, still talking to himself. Humans were so strange. It had lived around them all its life and yet it often felt no nearer to understanding them.

It shrugged and turned its attention once more to the blackberry.

Around the bend, Jem stopped. The light was beginning to drain from the sky; he ought to go home; his mother didn't like him to linger on the way back. But he had no choice – he might never get a chance like this again. There had been something close by – he knew it. It might have been a fox or a rabbit but neither of those animals, to the best of Jem's knowledge, ever sang.

Jem put down his bag, hesitating. Could it be true? Did a nouka still live in the hill? He had to find out, once and for all. He kicked off his shoes, he peeled off his socks, he unzipped his coat and flung it down. He needed to be able to move without making any noise at all.

The hill felt cool and pleasantly prickly under his bare soles, the ground firm, pushing up into the arches of his feet. His steps were careful, swift and silent, his feet making imperceptible whispers against the grass. He was aware of air entering and leaving his

lungs, the tick-tick of his pulse in his ears, and the feel of the breeze as it blew towards the hill and parted itself to travel around it.

Near the nettle patch, he dropped to all fours. Something was on the other side of these nettles. Jem knew it. He crept on his hands and knees up to the nettles, placing one stealthy palm in front the other, and then leant around them. It was going to be here. It was, it was.

Nothing. The only things behind the nettles were mud, rabbit droppings and some pebbles. Jem sank back to his heels. He had been so sure, so convinced that there had been something there.

He was just about to stand up, to return to life and normality, to face the fact that there was, indeed, no such thing as the nouka, when there was a slight but distinct rustle. A few feet away the bracken swayed, as if something was moving through it.

Jem listened, alert, straining his ears.

There it was again: a minute flicker of sound.

Jem edged forward, slithering on his stomach. His fingers gripped the soil, his forehead parting the undergrowth in front of him, his toes pushing against the ground, propelling him forward. The world felt enormous and minuscule, all at the same time. He was aware of the old volcano below him and the immense sky above him. He could see tiny insects clinging to grass stems, beetles toiling over grit in their path, a dropped feather covered with pearls of dew. Bracken and soil and twigs were filling his hair, his clothes, his nails. It seemed suddenly impossible to say where he ended and the hill began, as if his edges were blurring and dissolving, as if he were merging with what was around him.

He breathed in the scent of earth, of rock, edging forwards, easing aside the grass. He had no idea if he was heading in the right direction or if he was going up or down the hill, and whether there was anything at all to be seen here, but he kept going.

Then something so small but so extraordinary happened that the Earth seemed to stop turning, just for a moment.

FROM AMONG THE CRISS-CROSSING STALKS OF bracken in front of his face, appeared five tiny fingers. They were black and furred, with shiny apple-pip nails, and curled around a stem with a tentative grip.

The air seemed to leave Jem's chest; his limbs wouldn't work, as if he was a boy turned into stone.

The bracken parted, a small face appeared, and there it was. Verity's nouka.

Neither of them moved.

The nouka's eyes glistened in the half-light like two green moons, its fur stiffened and puffed up, making it look bigger than it really was.

Jem kept himself very still. He didn't take his eyes off the nouka. He didn't even know if he was breathing.

"Hello," he heard himself say, in a low voice.

The nouka didn't reply, didn't give any hint that it had even heard.

"I'm Jem. I live in the cottage. Over there. You …
you've been to visit us, haven't you?"

It blinked rapidly but still made no sound.

"It's OK," Jem added quickly. "We don't mind. We …
we like it when you come."

As soon as these words left his mouth, Jem knew
them to be true.

"Are you…?" Jem wondered what it was he wanted
to say. "Are you all right? You sounded … I mean, your
song sounded sad."

He thought for a moment. "I'm sorry. For saying you
didn't exist. And for stamping on your hill."

The nouka's ears flicked back and forth. It tugged at its whiskers, still gripping the bracken with one paw, regarding Jem with its unfathomable emerald gaze.

Carefully, carefully, Jem stretched out an arm. It did not enter his mind that he was a boy who fell off chairs, who broke things by accident, who made a mess of his schoolwork, who tripped over his own feet. Being there, with the nouka, who hadn't been seen for hundreds of years, had bestowed on Jem all the grace and poise and control of his limbs that he'd ever wanted.

He reached towards the nouka, closer and closer. All he knew was that he wanted to touch it, just once, to make contact, to stroke that dark silken fur. He had the feeling it would be as soft as thistledown.

The nouka watched, darting quick, beady looks from Jem's face to his hand and back again. His fingers were very close now and the nouka regarded them with curiosity, its head on one side.

Then an astonishing thing happened. It removed its paw from the bracken and, slowly, slowly, it took Jem's index finger. Its touch was delicate and strong, gentle and fierce, at once thrilling and infinitely reassuring.

The skin on its palm radiated a surprising heat and was as smooth as planed wood.

The next moment, it let go, and quick as an arrow shot from a bow, it turned and darted away through the undergrowth. And the nouka was gone. Jem stumbled upright, saying, "Wait, please come back!" but it was nowhere to be seen.

There was only Jem, the sky, the grass, and the sight of what appeared to be many, many rabbit holes leading away into the hill. Jem knelt down and looked into one, then another, then another.

"I'm going to go home to get my sister," he shouted into one. "Can you hear me?" he called into another. "I'm going to fetch Verity and then I'm coming back. I've got a surprise for you."

Then he turned and ran, leaving behind an empty hill and a startled silence.

As Jem sprinted towards the cottage, he could see Verity, busy tunnelling into the ground near the fence. His mother was near by, taking down washing from the line. He hurtled the final few yards, zigzagging down the path.

"Verity!" Jem shouted, as he came through the garden gate. "I need you. Come quick!"

Verity looked up, taken aback, and in that moment Jem realized how long it had been since he'd asked her to do anything with him. But she flung aside her trowel and ran towards him.

"Come where?" she said.

He pointed behind him. "Up there," he said, breathlessly,

"Mum, can we have a fire? At the top of the hill?"

His mother was surveying him, perplexed. "What's happened to you? You're covered in filth and—"

"Please can we have a fire?" He fastened his arms around her and gave her a tight squeeze. "Please? It's really important."

"I don't think so, sweetheart," she began. "It's a school night and there's this laundry to fold and—"

From behind them came a sound, as if a sudden breeze was threading itself through a thin pipe or tunnel, or as if someone was pulling a stick against a railing.

His mother looked thoughtful for a moment. Then she smiled and Jem knew that it was a yes-smile and a curious feeling spread from the place on his index finger where the nouka had touched him, up his arm, across his shoulder, throughout his ribcage, to the region of his heart. It felt like the thaw of ice after a long winter, like the release of water from a blocked tap. Jem shuddered with the unfamiliarity and relief of it.

His mother went into the house, and when she came back again, she was carrying her coat, a rucksack and a box of matches. She took Verity and Jem by the hand and the three of them began to climb up the side of the hill.

"We need to find firewood," Jem said, as they got higher and higher. "Lots of it. As much as we can."

"Why do we need this fire, Jem?" Verity asked, panting along beside him. Their mother was further ahead, carrying the wood.

"For the nouka," Jem said.

Verity stopped in her tracks. "The nouka?"

Jem grinned. "Yes. It's always doing things for us, isn't it? Causing chaos, giving us a bit of excitement, making us less dull. Cheering us up. So maybe it's time someone returned the favour."

She gave him a very puzzled look. "But you don't believe in the nouka. You said—"

the nouka are here.

92

"I've changed my mind," Jem said, picking up a stick and weighing it in his hand. "I'm sorry, Verity. I should take more notice of what you say." He glanced about him before bending over and whispering the following three words into her ear: "I saw it."

Verity gripped his sleeve, tipping back her head so that she could look him in the face. "You did?"

"Yes."

"Really?"

"Really."

"Did it look like the old lady said? Fluffy and black?"

"It did."

"Was it very, very lovely?"

Jem nodded. "It held my finger, just for a second or two."

Verity beamed, then hugged him tightly round the middle. One of the best things about his little sister, Jem thought as they stood there, was that she was never cross with him for long. "I wish I'd seen it," she muttered fervently into his jumper. "I wish I'd been with you."

"Me too. But now you can help me. And who knows? Maybe it will come out again. I have a feeling that it might be a bit lonely."

They kept climbing until they reached the very top of the hill, where there was a hollow, sheltered from the wind, filled with lush, verdant grass. Below them, they could see the village, spread out before them, the tiny houses huddling around the hill's base like gifts around a Christmas tree.

"This used to be the crater, when this hill was a volcano," Jem told Verity, and she knelt down and patted her hands against the soft earth, as if trying to conjure its ancient heat.

They set about building a fire with all the sticks and branches they had collected, small ones at the centre and large ones at the edge. The sun sank down in the sky and darkness pooled in all the dips and hollows of the hill.

As their mother struck a match and held it to the fire's base, Jem and Verity ran races around the rim of the crater. They watched a fingernail sliver of moon carve itself into the ink-dark sky; they saw the lights come on, one by one, all over the village. The flames of the fire caught easily and soon the crater was filled with writhing yellow flames, and for the first time in thousands of years, smoke could be seen rising from the summit of the old volcano.

When the fire was burning at its brightest, they came to huddle around it, Verity on their mother's knee for safety, with Jem next to them. Their mother opened her rucksack and brought out sandwiches, a flask and chocolate biscuits. They stared into the leaping flames, each seeing something different, and every time a log split open, a small shower of sparks burst upwards and then fell back to the ground.

Jem leant his head against his mother's shoulder, feeling for the first time in ages no desire to tap his feet or shift his legs, but instead a deep need to be exactly where he was.

"I like it here," he said.

"Do you?"

"Yes. Let's never move again."

Somewhere in the darkness behind him, Jem thought that he heard something. Like a rustle or a sigh or perhaps the flex of a branch. But he wasn't entirely sure. What he did know, however, was that when he reached for the biscuits he'd placed on the stone next to him, there was nothing there but a scattering of crumbs.

When they left later that evening, trailing back down the hill, the embers were still glowing orange and red against the dark sky, and Jem and Verity were sure, just for a moment, that they saw the outline of a small figure, arms outstretched to the heat. The remains of the fire were still crackling, still giving out sparks here and there, which rose up into the air like the coronet sprays of fireworks. Every time this happened, the figure leapt, clapping its little hands in delight.

AFTER THIS, LIFE BESIDE THE HILL WAS NEVER quite as peaceful as before.

Strange things continue to happen in most houses, all over the village. Bathroom sinks are found, sometimes, filled with wriggling tadpoles. Dogs wake to discover ribbons tied to their tails. Salt cellars have their contents switched for sugar. Nobody minds, or at least not much. People just shrug and say, "Perhaps a nouka was here last night."

Every year, just as summer begins its slow tilt towards autumn, the whole village climbs the hill and builds a huge bonfire at the top. It is known in these parts as Nouka Day. When the blaze is burning at its hottest, the people gather around the crater with mugs of hot chocolate. At the end of the evening, they walk back down the hill to their homes, leaving the glowing embers for others to enjoy.

The following morning, without fail, Jem and Verity will find something left on their doorstep: a pair of conkers still in their bristling green jackets, a red-gold leaf filled with acorns, or a piece of charcoal taken from the centre of a fire. They never see who leaves these gifts but there are always little footprints — a great many of them — leading back to the lower slopes. There the trail vanishes.

Verity and Jem go out most evenings, searching for noukas, and for their little vents and tunnels into the hill. They have yet to find them.

For all I know, they are looking
for them still.

tops and the roots

we are the roots of an older mommory that of its own,
and a tired presence hidden to the unknown, so and so.
we are the apple and orın in a breeze,
so the brain roots of oracle under a breeze.
we are the twentle of mean upon a pearls ralle,
and the years of a rest tight sleep in a kealle.
we are the house of a hundred chambers sat of its teal,
and the bigedin of a test branmons sleep in the meal.
we are the every of water behind an sats tante,
and the notes of a tops in the throat of a fante.

when stone is not stone
and a hill not a hill,
when a mountain breathes mist
and all sings with brook hill,
the roots are waking;
the roots are here.
always be certain:
the roots are near.

108

ye are the flush on a thrush in a thistle,
and the bush on a branch where once but a little.
ye are the burrow on an owl in the blue-midnight air,
and the tread on a otter coming late to her hair.
ye are the brim on a twist breaking under your nest,
or the third in the marketplace with a butter on best.
ye are the crossword clue on a plant to the bin,
and the hungry heart on a hare when it's race has been win.
ye are the sleet that on an otter alone her march,
and the blister sheen on the tried on a truck.

when stone is not stone
and a hill not a hill,
when a mountain breathes fire
and all stirs with black will,
the nights are waiting;
the nights are here.
always be certain,
and please never fear:
the nights are listening
and the nights are near.

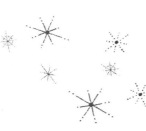

Song of the Nouka

We are the crack of an acorn popping out of its cup,

And a bird winging high to the clouds, up and up.

We are the ripple of corn in a breeze,

Or the sharp crack of icicles after a freeze.

We are the tremble of rain upon a leaf's edge,

And the weave of a nest built deep in a hedge.

We are the force of a flower bursting out of its bud,

And the squelch of a boot stamping deep in the mud.

We are the draw of water behind an oak's bark,

And the notes of a song in the throat of a lark.

When stone is not stone

And a hill not a hill,

When a mountain breathes fire

And all skies with smoke fill,

The noukas are waking;

The noukas are here.

Always be certain:

The noukas are near.

We are the plash of a frog in a brook,

And the sway of a branch where once sat a rook.

We are the screech of an owl in the blue-midnight air,

And the tread of a vixen coming late to her lair.

We are the snap of a twig breaking under your foot,

Or the thud in the fireplace with a scatter of soot.

We are the blissful turn of a plant to the sun,

And the frantic heart of a hare when its race has been run.

We are the sleek coat of an otter diving for perch,

And the silvery sheen on the trunk of a birch.

When stone is not stone

And a hill not a hill,

When a mountain breathes fire

And all skies with smoke fill,

The noukas are waking;

The noukas are here.

Always be certain,

And please never fear:

The noukas are listening

And the noukas are near.

When stone is not stone And a hill not a hill When a

moun-tain breathes fi-re And all skies with smoke fill The nou-kas are waking The

nou-kas are here   Al-ways be cer-tain The   nou-kas are near